It was so snowy one Christmas Eve,
we thought that Connor's train
would have to be cancelled.
He would need help from his
friends to pull home the
last train in time
for Christmas ...

First published in Great Britain 2017 by Farshore
This edition published in Great Britain 2021 by Dean
An imprint of HarperCollins*Publishers*
1 London Bridge Street, London SE1 9GF
www.farshore.co.uk

HarperCollins*Publishers*
1st Floor, Watermarque Building, Ringsend Road, Dublin 4, Ireland

 Thomas the Tank Engine & Friends ™

CREATED BY BRITT ALLCROFT

HiT entertainment

Based on the Railway Series by the Reverend W Awdry.
© 2018 Gullane (Thomas) LLC. Thomas the Tank Engine & Friends and
Thomas & Friends are trademarks of Gullane (Thomas) Limited.

© HIT Entertainment Limited. HIT and the HIT logo are trademarks of HIT Entertainment Limited.

PB ISBN 978 0 0084 9474 2
5 book set ISBN 978 0 0085 0015 3
10 book set ISBN 978 0 0084 9794 1
Printed in Great Britain.
001

A CIP catalogue record for this title is available from the British Library.

Stay safe online. Farshore is not responsible for content hosted by third parties.

Farshore takes its responsibility to the planet and its inhabitants very seriously.
We aim to use papers from well-managed forests run by responsible suppliers

The Last Train for Christmas

Based on
The Railway Series
by the
Rev. W. Awdry

Illustrations by
Robin Davies

DEAN

It was Christmas Eve on Sodor, and Thomas and Oliver were busy clearing snow from the tracks.

"I'm glad we won't have to wear our snow ploughs tomorrow," said Thomas. "We'll be warm in our Sheds instead!"

Oliver looked puzzled.

"Tomorrow is Christmas Day. No trains will run all day!" Thomas explained.

"Hurrah!" Oliver cheered.

Over on the Mainland, Connor was collecting passengers for Sodor. But there were too many people and Connor's coaches were soon full.

As the Guard waved his flag for Connor to go, there were still lots of people left on the platform.

"Don't worry, I'll be back," Connor promised. "There's still one more train before Christmas!"

The Fat Controller met Connor at Knapford.

"Sir, I need more coaches to make one last run to the Mainland and back. I'll bring everyone home in time for Christmas!" said Connor.

"Quickly then, Connor. The snow is getting heavier," The Fat Controller replied.

"Don't worry, Sir – I'm a **Really Fast Engine!**"
Connor smiled.

Connor steamed to the Yard for more coaches, but all he could see were three mounds of snow.

Suddenly, Thomas appeared, and with a **biff** of his buffers, all the snow fell away!

"Take these special **slip coaches**," Thomas said. "You can uncouple them without having to stop."

"I'll be quicker than ever!" Connor smiled.
And he hurried away.

Later, The Fat Controller had bad news. "Snow has blocked the Main Line," he said. "No more trains will run tonight."

"But Connor and his passengers need to get home for Christmas, Sir!" said Thomas.

"You're right," said The Fat Controller. "We must clear the tracks for Connor's last train."

"We'll do it together!" the engines agreed.

Thomas and Percy got straight to work, clearing snow along the Main Line up to Wellsworth. Suddenly, Percy spotted something in the sky.

"Look, Thomas!" Percy said excitedly. "Do you think it's Father—"

"It's Harold!" Thomas shouted. "He's searching for anyone stuck in the snow."

"Oh," sighed Percy.

Further down the line, the snow was very deep. Hiro was the only engine big and strong enough to help. He cleared the track just in time for Connor's train to pass!

"Peep! Peep! Thank you!" Connor called.

Hiro looked up at the sky. "Is that Father—?
Oh no, it's Harold on his patrol."

Connor released the first slip coach at Kellsthorpe Station. It rolled to a stop at the platform. Instead of waiting for the passengers to get off the train, Connor could set off straight away.

"Peep! Peep!" whistled James. "What clever coaches you have, Connor!"

Connor whooshed on, and released the second slip coach at Maron Station.

Thomas had just finished clearing the line at Wellsworth when Connor raced through.

Connor released the last slip coach, but this one rolled straight past the station!

"Fizzling fireboxes! The passengers will be stuck in the snow!" cried Thomas.

Thomas called Harold to help, and together they brought the coach back to the platform.

"Well done, Connor!" cheered The Fat Controller, as the big engine pulled into Knapford.

"Thank you, Sir!" Connor smiled. "But I couldn't have made it without my friends!"

"That's right," said The Fat Controller. "You **all** helped bring the last passengers home in time for Christmas!"

"**Peep! Peep!**" the engines whistled together.
"**Merry Christmas!**"

The engines were glad to puff back to their Sheds after a very busy Christmas Eve.

"**Merry Christmas**, Harold!" Thomas yawned, as a shape flew high above them.

But Harold was already fast asleep at the Search and Rescue Centre! Someone else was flying through the starry sky that night . . .

More about Connor

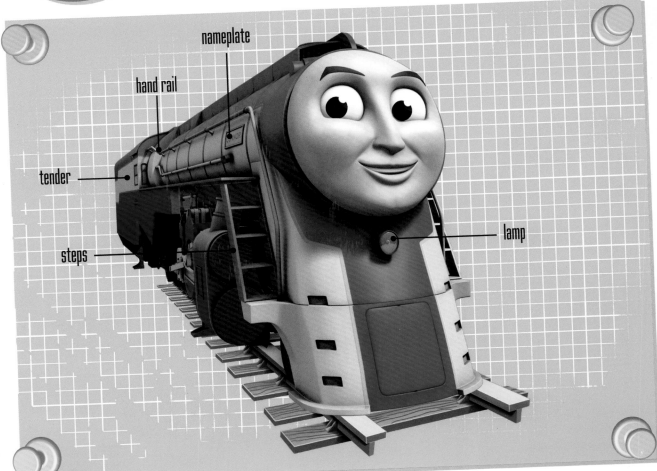

nameplate

hand rail

tender

steps

lamp

Connor's challenge

Look back through the pages of this book
and see if you can spot:

Christmas tree

moon

Father Christmas

lamppost

little boy